Emma Thomson's
Felicity Wishes

Viking
Published by Penguin Group
Penguin Young Readers Group
345 Hudson Street
New York, New York 10014

FELICITY WISHES
Text by Emma Thomson

Illustrated by Emma Thomson

With thanks to Emma Layfield and Helen Bailey

10 9 8 7 6 5 4 3 2 1

First published in Great Britain in 2003 by
Hodder Children's Books, a division of Hodder Headline Limited.
First published in U.S.A. in 2004 by Viking,
a division of Penguin Young Readers Group.

Printed in China

ISBN: 0-670-03682-X

Emma Thomson's

felicity Wishes

Little book of

Everyday Wishes

VIKING

January

Happy New Year!

1st

Stay happy and really believe in your dreams this year.

2nd

Take a deep breath and make a sparkling wish for a brand-new year.

3rd

Wish for fun and happiness the whole year through.

4th

Wake up from your dreams
with a smile, and your wishes may come true.

5th

Snuggle up by the fire and make a warm
winter wish.

6th

Make a quick wish in the next 30 seconds...
starting now!

7th

Point your nose in the direction of
your dreams and wish!

Make a wish first thing in the morning
and last thing at night. Double wishes!

9th

On a rainy day, wish for sunshine
and warmth.

10th

Close your eyes, quietly listen to your dreams,
and make a wish.

11th

In a dizzy moment, make a silly, giddy wish!

12th

Hold hands with your best friend and say your
wishes together at the same time.

13th

Make a wish when you see a bird
and it may just come true.

14th

Dance all your winter blues
away with a sunny, happy wish!

15th

On a perfect day, make a perfect wish.

16th

Send a get-well wish to
a sick friend.

17th

Make a wish that makes you feel warm
from your nose to your toes!

18th

Close your eyes, stretch out your arms,
and make a huge wish.

19th

Look for the blue in the sky and make a wish.

20th

When the wind blows, run in its direction
and make a wish.

21st

Stand on your tiptoes and make a
wish for something yummy.

22nd

On an ordinary day, make an
extraordinary wish!

23rd

This is the day for surprises.
Make a wish you never dreamed would come true!

Delicious!

Grant yourself a super, fantastic,
great hair day!

Catch a raindrop on the tip of your
tongue, count to ten, and make a wish!

You look so good!

Concentrate hard, wrinkle your forehead,
and make a wish.

Stand still for a moment and think about
today's wish. What will it be?

28th

Sleepovers, midnight feasts, and cozy chats—
make a friendship wish come true!

29th

On a gray day,
wish for the sun.

30th

When your head is in the clouds, make a wish
and you might end up on cloud nine!

31st

Wrap up warm and wish for
lots of warm things.

February

1st

Dance till you drop and make a fun-filled wish!

2nd

Close your eyes, count to ten and make a special wish!

3rd

Make a friendship wish for your very best friend.

4th

Skip to the top of a hill and sing your wish
to the world.

5th

Make a wish as you walk with your
hands in your pockets.

6th

If you sneeze three times, make a wish on
the third sneeze!

7th

Try to make your wishes
come true by really believing in your dreams.

When things are looking gray and cloudy...
wish for sunshine and blue skies.

Treat yourself to an extra special wish today.
What will it be?

Grant yourself a day of chocolate!

Stand out and make a wish that is a little
bit different!

Make a wish on a moonlit
sky...for the happiest
dreams tonight!

Giant sushi!

As you write your Valentine's Day card,
make an extra special wish
for your Valentine.

Wear something red and wish for love—
it's Valentine's Day!

My heart's all a-flutter!

15th

Seal a letter with a wish and a kiss.

16th

When you see a bird, stand on your tiptoes...
and make a wish!

Surprise yourself and make a dazzling wish
you never expected to make.

Make a wish for a super, smiley day.

Turn your daydreams into real dreams
by making a wish!

Make a special wish for someone close
to your heart.

When the phone rings, make a quick
wish before you answer it!

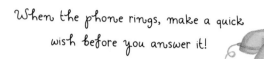

22nd

Make a wish as soon as you open your sleepy
eyes in the morning.

23rd

Find somewhere quiet and make a secret
wish just for you!

24th

Tap your toes, smile, and make a special wish.

Wish for Spring to come soon.

If you need a friend, make a wish for
one to be there.

Make a happy wish for
a happy day!

Make a wish to be a fairy for the day!

If it's a leap year, make a leaping wish!

March

1st

It's springtime.
Make a wish on a butterfly.

2nd

Spread a little happiness and make a wish
for each of your friends.

3rd

Grant yourself a day full of yummy things!

Make a wish to follow your dreams, and
who knows what could happen!

Make a wish just before you close your
eyes at night. Goodnight!

Stop and think about today's wish.
What will you wish for?

Blink three times, spin around,
and make a wish.

8th

Wish for a day where the fairies do all your work!

9th

Plant a seed, make a wish, and watch it grow!

10th

Get up early and make a wish before the sun rises.

11th

Make a brave wish for something you never dared to wish for before.

12th

Spring clean your wish list and
make a fresh, new wish.

13th

Find a four-leafed clover and make a wish.

14th

Whisper today's wish three times
and it may come true.

15th

Make a wish when you cut a
slice of yummy chocolate cake.

Add a little sparkle to your life...
Make a dazzling wish!

Make a special wish and send it to
your favorite person!

Remember to keep today's
wish a secret. Shhhh!

Chocolate brownies, Key lime pies, and
strawberry cake. Wish for them all!

Make a happy wish as soon as you wake
up in the morning.

21st

Make a silly, sunny,
funny, upside-down wish.

22nd

Wink at the moon and
make a glowing wish.

23rd

Make a wish on the
first spring flower you see.

Things look good from here!

24th

Grant yourself a day of fun, fun, fun! Enjoy!

25th

Spin round and round, and make a dizzy
wish on your third turn.

26th

As the first snowdrops appear,
make a gentle wish.

27th

Make a sunny wish even when it rains!

28th

Five, four, three, two, one...Wish!

29th

Wish on a star and watch the
night stars twinkle to make it
come true.

30th

A little piece of magic may just
come true if you make a wish today.

31st

Make a big wish and don't
forget anything!

I hope your wish comes true!

April

1st

One perfect white cloud in a blue sky
means one perfect wish might come true!

2nd

Take three deep breaths and wish
all your worries away.

3rd

Make a wish for everyone you know.

Make a wish
for a rainbow.

Fill today with lots of special wishes for
your friends and family.

Give someone a huge hug and make a wish
just for them!

Reach out and make a wish in the bright,
glittery sunshine.

Make a wish to be filled with peace
from your nose to your toes.

Take a walk in the sunshine or in the rain
and make a wish.

Wish to make someone
smile today.

Eeny, meeny, miny mo.
What will you wish for today?

Grant yourself an hour
in a relaxing bubble bath.

When things seem a little mixed-up,
make a wish to unscramble them!

Wish for all the things you love,
and then some more!

Don't tell anyone your secret wish today
or it might not come true!

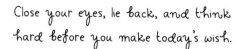

16th

Close your eyes, lie back, and think
hard before you make today's wish.

17th

Make this the day for
lots of fun wishes!

ADMIT
ONE
FAIRY

18th

Walk through the woods and
make a wish on a beautiful flower.

19th

When the moon smiles at you,
smile back and make a wish!

20th

When you are down in the dumps,
wish for happy days.

21st

Spin round three times one way and then
three times the other way. Wish!

22nd

Write down today's wish and
remember to keep it secret!

23rd

Throw a daisy into the wind
and make a wish as you let go.

This wish is for you!

Take a giant step and make a huge wish.

Make a wish for something special...
and it might just come true!

Make a wish with a best friend over a frothy,
creamy milkshake.

Be your own person and make
a special wish just for you!

28th

Wish on a star and let
your dreams shine brightly.

29th

Jump up and down three
times, spin round and
round twice, and wish!

You can do it!

30th

Make a wish
for someone you love.

May

1st

Whisper today's wish so
no one can hear.

2nd

Close your eyes tight and wish hard.
Your wish may just come true!

3rd

Wishes come true when you least
expect them to... Make a wish!

Sing a silly, funny wish to yourself.
Enjoy!

 Throw a coin into water
and make a wish!

Blue skies, green fields, yellow buttercups—
wish on something beautiful.

Wish on a bird carrying a
flower in its beak.

Make a wish on a white cloud and
it may just come true!

Help your wishes come true by
following the path they lead.

Stand on your head and
make a topsy-turvy wish!

As the clock chimes twelve,
make a striking wish!

When you see a shooting star, make a twinkly wish.

13th

Treat yourself and make a yummy
wish that's good enough to eat!

14th

Repeat today's wish three times
and it may just come true.

15th

Irresistible!

Smile as soon as you wake up,
and make a happy wish.

16th

Make a wish on the most beautiful flower
for a blossoming day.

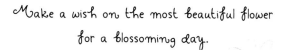

17th

Click your heels together three times
and make a wish.

18th

Make a wish for someone who is
always there for you. They deserve it!

19th

Look in the mirror and
make a wish just for you!

If you want your dreams to come true,
you have to make a wish!

21st

Tie a piece of string around your
little finger and make a wish.

22nd

Hold something you love close to
your heart, and make a wish.

23rd

Visit a friend—and make
a friendship wish together.

24th

Spend five minutes thinking about
a special wish for today.

25th

Hop on one leg, do five star jumps, and
make an energetic wish!

26th

Fairy cakes, chocolate brownies, and apple turnovers—
wish for lots of yummy things!

27th

Make a wish on the first beautiful
thing you see in the morning.

28th

Oops! Don't forget to
make a wish today!

29th

Dream larger, wish harder, and
your wishes may just come true.

So many wishes, so little time!

30th

Make a big wish for the world.

31st

Cross your fingers and toes for good luck
and then make a wish.

Summer

June

1st

Wherever you go or whatever you do,
make a wish to brighten up your day.

2nd

On a special day make an extra
special wish for happiness.

3rd

Red, yellow, violet, and green—make a rainbow wish!

Take all the time in the world
to make today's wish.

Close your eyes and visit the place
where dreams come true. Wish!

Spread a little sparkle and make
wishes for all of your friends.

Make a wish for your most
fabulous dream to come true.

When things are a little dull, make a silly,
funny wish to brighten up your day.

9th

Take a giant leap and make a giant wish!

10th

Make a wish for perfect
picnic weather.

11th

Spoil yourself and make a wish
for yummy things!

12th

When you have butterflies in your belly
and your legs have turned to jelly, make a wish.

13th

Make a wish on all the beautiful
things around you.

14th

Wish for fun and laughter, and
enjoy the rest of the day.

15th

Sniff the petals of a pretty pink rose
and make a wish.

16th

Make a tiny wish in a whisper for
something big and loud!

17th

Make a wish from the tips of your fingers
to the bottom of your toes.

18th

Stand on one leg, hop three times,
and make a silly wish!

19th

Take a break and make
today's wish.

When things look a little scary, wish for
all your troubles to go away.

When you see a flower in full bloom,
make a blossoming wish.

Make a wish, and who knows
what will come true!

Balloons, streamers and cake—make a party wish!

24th

Take a walk in the sunshine and smile
when you make today's wish.

25th

Pick the brightest flower you can find...
and make a wish!

26th

Wish for something you've always wanted,
and it might just come true!

27th

Make the ordinary extraordinary
with just one wish!

Send a sad friend a happy wish.

Make a wish
when you open
the front door for a
wonderful day.

A tiny wish is just as
powerful as a big wish!

I wonder what it will be?

July

1st

Whenever you need a friend,
close your eyes and make a wish.

2nd

Wish for something
you never wished for before.

3rd

An ice-cold drink, suntan lotion and ice cream—
make a summer wish!

Bonfires, fireworks, sparklers—
make a glittering, colorful wish.

Wish for a bit of fairy magic
to come your way.

Make a wish and follow it
wherever it may lead.

If you see a butterfly on a summer's day,
make a wish as it flutters by.

Sit among the flowers and the trees,
and make a beautiful wish.

There are lots of yummy things in life—
wish for them all!

When you need a lift, make a sunny wish to
brighten up your day.

Picnics, hazy days, and warm sun—
make a summer wish!

12th

Catch up with a friend and make a wish
over a yummy, frothy milkshake.

13th

Make an extra-special wish for someone
close to your heart.

14th

Make a wish for all your favorite things...
just not at the same time!

15th

As you lick the drips off your ice cream cone,
make a summery wish.

16th

Jump up and down three times,
turn around twice, and make a wish!

17th

Sit back, relax, and wish away!

18th

Lie in the warm summer grass and whisper
your wish to yourself.

19th

Wish for good things and they may come true!

20th

Don't get distracted—let the phone ring and make your wish in peace.

I'm busy wishing!

21st

Wish for two of your favorite things in one wish!

22nd

As you watch the sun go down, make a wish for another great day.

23rd

Make a silly, sunny, funny wish!

24th

Make a wish for a bit of magic
to come your way.

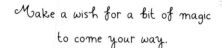

25th

Make a wish for all your favorite chocolate treats.

26th

Put on your brightest dress and
make a colorful, sparkly wish!

27th

Swap your favorite wish with your
best friend and see what happens.

28th

Surprise yourself
and make a fantastic wish!

29th

Make a special wish for
something you need.

30th

Make a wish for
ice-cold lemonade.

31st

Grant yourself a day
of being lazy!

August

1st

One, two, three, four...wish!

2nd

Close your eyes and whisper your wish to yourself.

3rd

Send a text-message wish to your fairy godmother.
It may just come true!

4th

Whenever you need a friend,
close your eyes and make a wish.

5th

Wish for a day full of special treats.

6th

Place the tip of your first finger on your nose
and make a secret wish.

7th

Sometimes wishes you don't mean
to make might just come true!

On a cloudy day,
make a wish for sunshine.

Everyone's different so be yourself
and make a wish especially for you!

Make a wish and remember
to keep it safe and secret.

Make a daisy chain and say
a wish every time you add a flower.

12th

Make a wish come true by
really believing it can happen.

13th

Close your eyes in the warm summer sun
and make a wish.

14th

Wish for your favorite treat.
It may just come true!

15th

Before you wish, stop and think about something
you've always dreamed of. Now wish!

16th

Bake a fairy cake and wish all
your worries away.

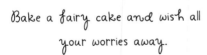

17th

Make an extra special wish for yourself
and your best friend.

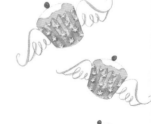

18th

Stand tall on your toes and wish for happiness!

19th

Make a wish each time you see a bird, and
let magic flutter into your heart.

20th

Make a wish as soon as you wake up
and it may come true today.

21st

It's summertime! Wish on the brightest flower
in your garden.

22nd

Make a wish for your favorite
dream to come true!

23rd

Get up early and make a happy wish
before the sun rises.

Clap your hands together three times
and make a wish.

Make a dazzling wish on a bright, sunny day.

Take a walk in the countryside
and tell a rabbit your wish.

Look high into the summer sky
and wish on a distant cloud.

28th

Red, yellow, green and blue—
make a colorful wish!

29th

Big, small, tiny—make a wish whatever the size!

30th

Make a wish and then another one!
Two wishes today!

31st

When you're feeling a little blue,
wish on something sunny.

Autumn

September

1st

Make a wish every day, and one day your wishes may come true.

2nd

Sit under an apple tree, catch a falling apple, and make a wish.

3rd

Make a wish for a dream to come true.

Dance around your garden
three times and make a wish.

Treat yourself to an extra-special wish today.
What will it be?

Count backward from ten, and when
you reach one, whisper your wish.

Write your wish down. Keep it in a
safe place, and one day your wish
might come true.

8th

Make yourself smile with a wish
for your dreams to come true.

9th

Bake a dreamy chocolate cake and
make a wish on the first gooey bite.

10th

Wish for a beautiful sunset.

11th

Wriggle your nose, think of a number
under ten, and make a wish!

12th

Make a wish for someone
close to your heart.

13th

Let the phone ring and quickly
make a wish before you answer it.

14th

Make a wish to forget about
your worries for one day.

15th

Take ten deep breaths and
slowly make today's wish!

16th

Wish on the stars for a dazzling day ahead.

17th

Even a little wish can go a long way,
so don't forget to make your wish today.

18th

Grant yourself a day of special treats.

19th

Make a wish for lots of
yummy things.

20th

Make a special, sparkly wish for your friends.

21st

Jump up and down three times and
make a wish in midair!

22nd

Lie on top of a hill, close your eyes tight
and make today's wish.

23rd

Sparkly makeup and magic hair
mousse—make a pampering wish!

24th

Decisions, decisions.
What will you wish for today?

25th

When you see your reflection in a puddle,
wish for something special.

26th

Make a magical wish for a magical day.

27th

When you're walking down the street,
make an everyday wish!

28th

Spend time with friends and family
and wish for lots of fun and smiles.

29th

Make a sunny wish on a rainy day
and let it brighten up your day!

30th

Spoil yourself and make a wish
just for you!

Bliss!

October

1st

Bake fairy cakes and make a wish when
you take the first bite!

2nd

Walk through a puddle and make a
big splash as you wish.

3rd

Treat yourself to a yummy wish!

Make a warm wish in a hot, steamy bath.

Share a wish with your friend and
make it come true together.

Chestnuts, golden leaves, and crisp mornings—
make an autumn wish.

Curl up and read a good book.
Make a wish as you turn
the last page.

When you are a little lonely,
make a wish for someone to be there.

Make a special fairy wish
for someone you love.

Hold on to your dreams and
remember to make your wish today.

Whisper your wish through your mailbox!

12th

Face mask, conditioner, and lots
of bubbles—treat yourself!

13th

Forget about your worries and make a wish!

14th

Make a wish to shop until you drop!

15th

Celebrate friendship and make a
wish with your best friends.

Make a wish quietly to yourself and maybe
it might just come true.

On a frosty morning, make a sparkly winter wish.

Make a special wish for
a perfect day.

On a cloudy day, put on your
favorite party dress and make
a colorful wish.

Put your hand on your heart and
make a wish for someone you care about.

Make all your wishes come true by really
believing in yourself.

It's autumn!
Make a wish on a golden leaf.

Hot chocolate, log fires, cozy blankets—
wish for lots of warm things.

24th

Stick your tongue out to catch a raindrop
and make a wish.

25th

When things are a little gray,
make yourself a silly wish.

26th

Hug someone dear to you and make a warm wish.

27th

Catch a falling leaf and make an autumn wish.

28th

Grant yourself a super, fantastic wish!

29th

Close your eyes, sink into a bubble bath,
and make your wish for today.

30th

Join hands with your friends
and make a friendship wish to last forever.

31st

Make a wish for a special Halloween treat.

November

1st

Make a warm wintry wish—just for you!

2nd

Wish on the brightest star in the sky and the night
stars might just shine for you.

3rd

Snuggle down in your favorite chair and really think
about today's wish.

4th

Wish on a falling snowflake, or a raindrop!

5th

Make a wish and
repeat it five times to yourself.
It may just come true!

6th

Make a wish for someone who
is always on your mind.

7th

Grant yourself a day of pampering!

8th

On a crispy, cold morning,
whisper your wish to a robin.

9th

On the first bite of yummy
chocolate cake, make a wish.

10th

Make a warm wish for someone
close to your heart.

11th

Send sparkly wishes to
your family and friends.

12th

Wrap up warm and go on a long wintry
walk to think about today's wish.

13th

Put on your party dress, do a little
dance, and make a party wish!

14th

If you need a shoulder to cry on,
make a wish for a friend to be there.

15th

Have fun today and make
a topsy-turvy wish!

I'm here!

Make someone smile today
and send them a wish.

Take a bath and make a splishy-splashy wish!

Stand on top of a hill
and let the wind blow your wish away.

Think hard about your dreams and
make a wish for them to come true.

Blink three times and make a special fairy wish.

Lie on your back, point your toes to the sky,
and make a wish!

Wish on something beautiful for a beautiful
wish to come true.

Cold nights, dark days—
wrap up warm and make a bright wish!

24th

In a dizzy moment,
make an upside-down wish.

25th

When you see the first snowflake of the year,
make a special wish!

26th

Send a friend who is sick
a get-well wish.

27th

Shower yourself with wishes today.
You deserve it!

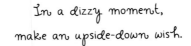

28th

Cold mornings, icy paths, and frosty trees—
make a wish on a wintry day.

29th

Forget about your worries and
make a new wish for a new day.

30th

Dance by the light of the moon
and wish for happy times.

Winter

December

1st

Log fires and fairy sing-alongs—
make a warm, wintry wish.

2nd

Write your wishes in a letter to Santa,
and who knows what will come true!

3rd

When you see a robin, stand on your tiptoes
and make a wish on its red breast.

4th

As the first snowflake falls, make a wish.

5th

When you make a Christmas cake,
stir the mixture with love and make a wish.

6th

Curl up in a chair and make a warm
wish from your toes to your nose.

7th

Let's party! Wish for an exciting day.

Mince pies, Christmas pudding, and
candy—wish for lots of yummy things!

When you see a snowman, make a wish.

Decorate your house and
make a tinselly Christmas wish.

Make a wish for those far away
from you at this special time of year.

12th

Fall over in the snow and make
a wish that no one sees!

13th

Be generous and make a wish
for the whole wide world!

14th

As you write your Christmas cards,
make an extra-special wish for your friends.

15th

When you put the first ornament
on the Christmas tree, make a wish.

16th

As you wrap your presents for the ones
you love, wrap a Christmas wish, too.

17th

Look at the fairy on top of the tree
and make a magical Christmas wish.

18th

Put on your party outfit
and make a sparkly wish.

19th

It's snowing!
Make a winter wonderland wish.

20th

Make a wish, wrap it in a snowball,
and throw it as far as you can.

21st

Treat yourself this Christmas
and make an extra wish!

22nd

Build a snowman, add eyes
and a nose, and make a wish!

23rd

Christmas is coming...Make a
wish for something special.

I wish I had a scarf like yours!

24th

Hang up your stocking, close your eyes,
and make a wish. Who knows what you will get?

25th

It's Christmas! Believe in the magic of
Christmas and let your wishes come true.

26th

Wish for a kiss under the mistletoe.

27th

Wish for peace.

Merry Christmas!

28th

Wish for a letter from a faraway friend.

29th

Catch a snowflake in your hand,
and make a wish before it disappears.

30th

Sprinkle wishes around your bedroom
for a dazzling day.

31st

As the clock strikes twelve,
make a magical wish for the New Year.

With this book comes a
special everyday wish:

Hold the book in your hands and
close your eyes tight.
Count backwards from ten and
when you reach number one, whisper
your wish...
...but make sure no one can hear.
Keep this book in a safe place and,
maybe, one day, your wish will come true.

Love,
felicity

x